MEG
AND THE
TREASURE
NOBODY SAW

MEG
AND THE
TREASURE
NOBODY SAW

ABOUT THIS BOOK

It all started with a violent summer storm—lightning, thunder, torrents of rain, and cyclone-force winds. Meg loved to watch storms, and if she hadn't watched this one, she might never have seen the mysterious figure in white entering the big, deserted Haywood house on the hill that night.

Being Meg, she had to find out what was going on at the big old house. Her friends Bud and Sally Haywood *had* told her to keep an eye on the place, *sort of.*

The trouble was that, when she did investigate, nobody would believe she had found muddy footprints—going in, but not coming out of, the Haywood front door—or that she had seen a face at an upstairs window—or that she had watched, *with her own eyes,* a third-floor window slowly being opened. And when she had solved the mystery, all by herself, she couldn't get help because she had promised not to tell!

But Meg does it again—comes through with the important clue to THE TREASURE NOBODY SAW!

Meg

AND THE TREASURE
NOBODY SAW

by Holly Beth Walker

illustrated by Cliff Schule
cover illustration by Olindo Giacomini

GOLDEN PRESS
Western Publishing Company, Inc.
Racine, Wisconsin

CONTENTS

1

BEST STORM OF THE YEAR

There was a big crash. Lightning filled the whole sky. The wind blew so hard that the great oak tree outside Meg's window tossed its branches like giant arms, this way and that. Meg could see that the heavy outdoor furniture had been blown over down below on the patio.

Meg, standing at her window in her pajamas, gave a little shiver of excitement. She loved storms. She loved feeling so safe in this big brick house. Why, this was more fun than watching the fireworks shows with her father when they had lived in Japan!

Meg knew a good way to tell how far off a storm

A MEG Mystery

was. All you had to do was count the seconds between the lightning and the thunder. She started counting when she saw the next ragged flash. She tried to make each count last one second, the way her father had told her to do.

"Mississippi one, Mississippi two, Mississippi three . . ." and then she heard the thunder. Three seconds—that meant three miles. That was lots farther away than the village of Hidden Springs.

Another flash showed her the house where Kerry Carmody, her best friend, lived. And off to the right she could see the big old Haywood house up there on the hill.

Downstairs she could hear the Wilsons shutting the windows. They didn't like storms one bit. They had this whole house to take care of, and storms meant extra work. Mrs. Wilson sometimes had curtains to wash. And Mr. Wilson's flower beds and the vegetable garden were always a mess after a big storm.

"Are you enjoying the storm, Meg?" It was her

father's voice behind her. He put her robe around her shoulders. "It's turned very cool for June."

"This storm's neat, Daddy. Stay here and watch it with me."

He touched her long, brown braids, the way he often did. Then he put his arm around her. She could feel the bigness of him. She could feel the rough terry cloth of his summer robe, which, she knew without looking, was white.

"Your mother loved storms." He said the words in that tone he often used when he spoke of her mother. "You're very much like her, Meg."

"I know." She pressed her cheek against his arm for a second. He had told her that a thousand times.

There was a flash of light and at the same instant a great crash. Meg grabbed her father's arm and hid her eyes for a moment. She wasn't afraid, really. But there hadn't been any time to count, and that meant the storm was right overhead.

He hugged her and laughed a little, as if he liked to have her hang on to him like that because she didn't do it very often. "That was a pretty close one, wasn't it?"

"Do you think it hit anything, Daddy?"

"No, I don't think so. But I'm glad to be in a safe house when it's that close. I'm glad we have lightning rods on the roof."

"Me, too."

"I want you to enjoy storms, Meg, and not be afraid. But I want you to know how to keep safe,

16

too. Never stand in a draft—that's why I always come in to be sure your windows are closed. Never stand on a porch in an electrical storm. And, of course, never stand under a big tree. I've told you all that.''

It sometimes seemed to Meg as if her father knew something about everything. She bet he knew as much as any of those important people he worked with in Washington. As much as the President, even!

He kissed the top of her head. ''Well, good night again, honey. I must go back to bed. I have to go in to work early tomorrow morning.''

At the doorway he turned. ''Where's Thunder?''

''He's on my bed.'' Meg glanced around to be sure. There the big Siamese cat lay. He probably hadn't even bothered to open his big blue eyes.

''Storms bore Thunder,'' she said.

''What a cat. He's not afraid of anything.''

Neither am I, really, thought Meg. *I just love things that are different and exciting.* Mrs. Wilson was always saying that her curiosity was going to get her into trouble. But it hadn't got her into any real trouble yet.

Another jagged streak of lightning split the sky. And before Meg got to "Mississippi two," the thunder crashed. She leaned toward the window, staring. She wiped away the mist her breath had made.

Why, that was strange. There was a car going up the lane to the Haywood house over there to the right on the hill. It was moving slowly, as if it could hardly make it. She could see the headlights through the trees. In the next flash of light, she could see the dark car itself.

Nobody was living at the Haywood house now. Bud and Sally Haywood had left for the summer to work and earn money so they could go to college in the fall. Their parents were dead. Bud had gone to work in Alaska in a fish-canning factory, and Sally had gone to Yellowstone Park. Surely they wouldn't be coming back so soon.

But the car had stopped at the big front porch. In the next flash, Meg saw what looked like a figure

in white moving up the steps.

Thunder jumped down from the bed and came to rub against her leg, purring. She picked up the big heavy cat, trying to stare through the storm.

But the rain was coming down very hard against the window now. She couldn't see the figure in white. She couldn't even see the car. And then the rain was so heavy that she couldn't see the Haywood house at all.

She went back to bed, cuddling Thunder close. She could feel his purring, as well as hear it. Thunder never purred for anyone but her.

He's a strange cat, she thought with satisfaction. *But he loves me, and I've nobody else to play with this summer.*

With Kerry Carmody away, it was going to be a terrible summer. Lucky Kerry. There were two girls and five boys in that family. Now the whole family was on a trip to California. They had a real bus, all fitted up with bunks and a kitchen and everything.

Meg yawned. She had promised to write to Kerry,

but there probably wouldn't be much to write about.

She shut her eyes. Had she really seen somebody in white going up the Haywood steps? Surely nobody would go around in white in a storm. But she had seen the car. That was for sure.

She was too sleepy now to think about it anymore. But tomorrow, first thing, she was going to go up there and see what she could find out.

2
THE FACE AT
THE WINDOW

The next morning, Meg woke to June sunshine and the song of birds. She lay for a while, looking around her pink and white room, feeling lazy. Then she remembered last night's storm. She jumped out of bed and put on blue jeans and a shirt. It might be a good idea to get out of doors and see if anything exciting had happened in the night.

"Margaret Ashley Duncan!"

Meg had just started to slip quietly out the front door when she heard her name. She turned. Mrs. Wilson stood at the other end of the hall, at the kitchen door.

"Surely you don't want to go out of the house without your breakfast!"

"I'm not hungry yet. Please, Mrs. Wilson. I just want to find out—"

"Oh, my, oh, my." The eyes behind the glasses were kind. "You're always wanting to find out something, Meg Duncan! Come now, your breakfast is all ready. Your father left for Washington an hour ago, but he expects me to see that you don't skip your meals."

While Meg ate her breakfast, Mrs. Wilson talked about the big storm. The rain had come in the living-room windows. The patio was covered with leaves and twigs. And the wind had knocked over all the furniture.

"I know," said Meg. "I stood and watched. I love storms."

"Oh, dearie me." Mrs. Wilson poured Meg another glass of orange juice. "Don't tell that to poor Mr. Wilson. It will probably take him all day to clean up the yard."

After breakfast Meg took Thunder in her arms and went to find Mr. Wilson. She saw the sun shining on his hammer as he was trying to put the rose trellis back in place.

She said politely, "We did need the rain, didn't we, Mr. Wilson?"

"Yes, but we didn't need the wind. And we didn't need a flood. The mailman told me that there are big tree branches down all over Kenilworth County. The Old Stone Bridge is out—it will be days before they get around to fixing it. And just look at my roses!"

Meg was sorry about the roses. She loved them, too. But she hoped she would never get too grown-up to love a storm.

First, she decided, she would go over to Old Bridge Road to see where the bridge was out.

Holly House, which belonged to Mrs. Partlow, was next door, and Meg cut across her lawn. Mrs. Partlow never minded, even though her gardener kept the grass like green velvet. Mrs. Partlow, for all

24

her years, was young in heart. Meg's father was always saying that.

"Hi, Mrs. Partlow." Meg waved at her elderly friend, whose white hair was shining like new snow. "How did you like that storm?"

"That was a beauty, wasn't it?" Mrs. Partlow laughed. "And see how pretty the grass looks after the rain!"

When Meg got to Old Bridge Road, she glanced toward the big Haywood house on the hill. In the bright sunlight, it looked quite different from the way it had looked in the storm.

She wished she knew whether or not she had really seen somebody in white going up onto the porch last night. But she did know she had seen a car, although there was no sign of car tracks in the lane now.

She was surprised when she got to the place where the bridge had been. Cricket Run wasn't much more than a brook usually. She and Kerry often walked across it on the stones. But now it was almost like

26

a little river. She threw sticks into the rushing water and watched them twist and turn as they were carried away. Thunder played and pretended to hunt in the fallen branches.

After a while, she called Thunder and started back. "I'll have to write Kerry and tell her about Old Stone Bridge being out," she murmured. "But that's not very exciting. Maybe I'll tell her about the figure in white."

She stopped at the end of the Haywood lane. Car tracks could have been washed away by the rain, of course. She looked up the long lane toward the house on the hill. There was no sign of a car there now.

The Haywood house was very big, with many rooms. It had white trimming, like wooden lace, all around the porches and windows. It was the only house in the area that wasn't kept up. But Bud and Sally Haywood didn't have any money.

I love Bud and Sally, Meg thought. *They're my friends, even though they are lots older than I am.*

27

They don't treat me like a baby.

"Keep an eye on the place for us, Meg," Sally had said when she left. Just the other day, Meg had received a card from her. It had a picture of the place in Yellowstone Park where she was working.

Meg picked up Thunder and started up the long lane. It wouldn't do a bit of harm to look around and make sure everything was all right.

There certainly wasn't much in the house worth stealing—or worth selling, either. Sally had decided that, sadly, just before she left. Meg remembered the strange little man who had come out from the antique shop in the city. He had come to look things over just before Sally went away.

He had held his shoulders all hunched up, and he hadn't been very polite. He just shook his head when he looked at the Haywood furniture. Meg remembered the way he had picked through the books, tossing one after another aside.

"Trash," he had said. "Just trash. Folks usually have to pay to have junk like this hauled away."

The Face at the Window

Sally hadn't liked that very much, and neither had Meg. There were some wonderful books in that house. Meg had been borrowing books there ever since she could remember.

The little man had said, "I'll give you fifty dollars for all this junk."

Meg remembered the way Sally's chin had gone up in the air. "I'll let you know if I decide to sell," she had said.

Sally's little dog had growled at the man when he was in the house going through the books. He had followed him out to the car, barking. And the man had picked up a stone and thrown it at him.

It was hot now, walking up that muddy hill. At the top of it, Meg stood looking up at the big house, with Thunder in her arms.

The house had looked spooky last night in the storm. But it didn't look a bit spooky now. Maybe what she had seen last night had been a bush blowing in the wind. A bush with white flowers. Or a tree.

She looked around. There was no tree or bush with white flowers on it.

But I wouldn't be afraid to go in there right now, she thought. *I could get some books to read. It would be perfectly all right with Bud and Sally.* Time and again they had told her to help herself to anything she wanted to read.

They were careless about locking doors. Meg knew it would have been just like them to go away for the whole summer without remembering to lock the doors. She listened for a minute and didn't hear anything. Well, she *was* supposed to look after the place, sort of.

She went over to the front porch. The house was so big that it made her feel very small. Thunder jumped down and ran into the bushes when she started up the brick steps.

At the top of the steps, she looked after him. Thunder had disappeared. He wasn't much protection, but she had felt better, somehow, with him held tightly in her arms.

"I guess I won't go in," she decided. "I'll just try the front door and make sure it's locked."

And then she saw something. She stood still, her eyes wide. There were muddy footprints on the porch floor. They went in the front door—and they didn't come out!

Meg took a step backward. Then she just flew down the steps. Somebody was in there! What if those footprints belonged to the strange little man who had thrown stones at Sally's dog?

As Meg ran down the muddy hill, she half expected to have a stone thrown at her. People who didn't like dogs probably didn't like children, either. And maybe they didn't like cats.

"Here, Thunder . . . kitty, kitty!"

She was at the bottom of the lane now, safe on Old Bridge Road. She could hear Mrs. Partlow's gardener mowing the grass. She could hear the sound of Mr. Wilson's hammer. But Thunder was nowhere in sight. That cat never did come unless he just happened to want to.

She started across the road, looking back over her shoulder to the Haywood house. And then she stopped, staring.

In one of the windows on the third floor, she saw something. She blinked. Those two rooms up there were where the servants' quarters used to be. And at one of the windows there seemed to be a face.

Yes, yes, she saw it clearly. There was a face at one of the windows!

3
WHY WON'T SOMEONE BELIEVE ME?

"I saw a face!" Meg was all out of breath from running. "Mr. Wilson, I saw a face at the Haywoods' window!"

Mr. Wilson put down the bushel basket of clippings. He mopped his forehead and his balding skull with a blue handkerchief. "My, it's hot. What's that, Meg?"

Meg was almost jumping up and down. "I saw a face at the Haywoods' window. Up on the third floor!"

"But Bud and Sally left a couple of weeks ago, didn't they?"

"Yes, yes. They told me to look after their house, sort of, and—"

"Sort of. Yes, I know." He smiled at her and started to pick up his basket.

"They did, Mr. Wilson! So I went up there this morning. Last night, you see, in the storm I thought I saw a—a figure in white—"

He gave her a look out of the corner of his eye.
. "Well, I *thought* I did. There was something. And I did see a car go up the drive. But just now I saw a face at the window on the third floor! And there were muddy footprints going in and not coming out!"

Mr. Wilson gave a sigh and started off with his basket.

Meg ran along behind him. "You have to believe me, Mr. Wilson."

"Oh, I do." He gave her a look over his shoulder that pretended to be serious. "You saw a ghost last night. The Haywood place is haunted!"

He was always teasing. "Oh, Mr. Wilson! I did

35

see that face in the window just now. Honest. Aren't you going to do anything about it?''

"Sure I am. Only let me empty this basket first."

Meg stayed right at his heels while he emptied the basket. Then she followed him into the kitchen. Mrs. Wilson was making a blueberry pie. She kept nodding, looking over her glasses at Meg while Mr. Wilson talked.

"Call Constable Hosey," she said.

"I hate to bother him. After this storm, he's got everybody for miles around calling him up."

Mrs. Wilson sprinkled sugar on top of her blueberries. "I know that. But Meg may really have seen somebody—"

"I did! Yes, I really did!" Meg nodded her head so hard her braids bounced. "I'm supposed to look after the place, sort of."

Mrs. Wilson gave her a smile. "And we are supposed to look after you, Margaret Ashley Duncan, but not just 'sort of.' Goodness' sake, child, it worries me to have you roaming around the Haywood

place, especially if there is any chance of somebody hiding there.''

"You're right," said Mr. Wilson. "That settles it. I'll call Constable Hosey.''

"Good." Mrs. Wilson lifted the top crust onto the pie and started to pinch the edges together.

"Oh, let me do that," Meg said. "Please, Mrs. Wilson.''

"All right. Wash your hands.''

Meg washed her hands, and then she pinched the edges of the piecrust together. It wasn't as easy as it looked, but it was fun. She could hear Mr. Wilson across the room at the kitchen telephone talking to Mr. Hosey.

Mrs. Wilson said, "That looks fine, Meg." She slid the pie into the hot oven. "You can tell your father at dinner tonight that you helped make the pie." She turned to Mr. Wilson, who was just hanging up the phone. "Well, what did he say?''

"He's as busy as a bird dog. But he said he'd try to stop by this afternoon.''

Late that afternoon, Meg was in her room. She had taken off the muddy jeans she had worn all day and had a bath. Her father liked to have her dress nicely for dinner.

Just as she was taking a pink dress from her closet, she heard a car drive in. She ran to the hall window and saw Mr. Hosey's car. It was black, with a star on the door. He didn't get out, and Meg knew that meant he was in a hurry.

"Well, I went up to the Haywood place," Mr. Hosey called across the lawn to Mr. Wilson. "I didn't see a sign of anything wrong."

Mr. Wilson went to stand by the car. He took out his pipe. "Good. I didn't really think you would, but we wanted to be on the safe side."

"Folks make it hard for the law when they go away and don't lock up their houses. Bud and Sally hadn't locked a single door. I put padlocks on the doors—not that padlocked doors will keep anybody out. There are at least twenty windows on the first floor that can be opened easy as pie."

39

"Did you see any tire tracks on the drive?"

"Nary a track. Of course, the rain could have washed them away. I did go in and look all around downstairs. I even looked around a bit on the second floor."

"Did you see any sign of footprints going in and not coming out?"

"No, not a one."

Both men laughed a little. Mr. Hosey started up his car. "It's probably just Meg's imagination."

"She's got plenty of that," said Mr. Wilson.

Upstairs, Meg went back to her room, thinking, *That's almost the same as saying I tell lies.* She thumped a pillow so hard on the window seat that two feathers flew out. *I saw a face at the window! I did, I did!*

Feeling cross, Meg put on her pink dress. She took her comb and brush downstairs and sat in the kitchen waiting until Mrs. Wilson could do her braids. She hated her braids. She wished her hair were short, like Kerry Carmody's, so she wouldn't

ever have to ask anybody to help her with it.

Mrs. Wilson brushed and braided with quick fingers. "Hold still, honey."

"I did see a face at the window, Mrs. Wilson." She turned to look up at Mrs. Wilson's face. "I really did."

"I'm sure you thought you did, Meg. You always tell the truth. Just hold still five seconds more . . . there, now. You look pretty and neat. Now let me get on with dinner."

Meg went to stand by Mrs. Wilson as she shelled green peas for dinner. She ate one of them, and it didn't taste very good. She said, "I can tell you don't really believe me. I'll never tell you anything else as long as I live."

Mrs. Wilson looked at Meg over her glasses. "My, oh, my." Her fingers were very fast. The peas rattled into the pan like little green bullets.

"Thieves and robbers can carry off all the furniture up there, and I'll never say one word to you. Or Mr. Wilson. Or Constable Hosey."

"Good." Mrs. Wilson's eye twinkled. "Now, listen, honey. Either set the table for me or go out and play."

Meg moved slowly into the dining room. She started getting the silver out of the chest. Somehow, just touching the silver made her feel better. The silver had belonged to her mother. It had her initials engraved on it.

She got out linen place mats, and they had her mother's initials on them, too. She placed the silver with care. And then she looked up at the portrait that smiled down at her from over the mantel.

Her mother's hair and eyes had been brown, just like Meg's. Her cheeks in the portrait were pink, and her dress was pink, like the dress Meg was wearing.

But a portrait, even in color, didn't tell you all you wanted to know. What had her voice sounded like, for instance? And would she have listened, really listened, when Meg told her something?

Yes. And Meg could imagine her voice. She could imagine how her mother would say, "You did?" not

43

even smiling. "You really saw a face—a person's face—in that window? And you saw footprints? Tell me all about it, Margaret Ashley, and don't leave out a single thing. . . ."

Later, at the dinner table, her father said, "They tell me you saw a face at the window of the Haywood house, punkin. And you saw footprints. Well, well." He looked across Meg's head to smile at Mrs. Wilson, who was coming in with the vegetables.

Meg lifted a shoulder. She flicked back a braid. *It was my story,* she thought. She had looked forward to telling her father all about it. And now they had told it first and spoiled it all.

Mrs. Wilson patted Meg's shoulder. "Guess who helped me make the blueberry pie you're going to have for dessert."

Pinching the edge of that old pie wasn't really helping, Meg thought. She took a sip of water, saying nothing. She was so tired of being treated like a baby!

When Mrs. Wilson had left the room, Meg's father said, "I know your feelings have been hurt, Meg. I don't doubt that you saw something—or thought you did. Sometimes our eyes play tricks on us. A cloud in the sky might be reflected in a window. Haven't you ever seen a face in a cloud?"

"Yes. But this wasn't a cloud." She took another sip of water, not looking at her father.

"All right. Suppose you tell me all about it. Start at the beginning."

Meg raised her eyes to her father's face. It was hard to stay mad at him. "All right. Last night I stood at my window after you left. And I saw a figure in white going up the steps of the Haywood house—"

He burst out laughing. "Oh, Meg, forgive me for laughing, but I just can't help it! That really must have been your imagination. You probably saw a bush waving in the wind or something illuminated by the lightning. But no ghosts!"

Meg felt almost like crying. But Meg never cried. She looked down at her plate, rolling the peas around with her fork. She frowned, as if the peas were very interesting.

Her father leaned to put his big hand over hers. He gave it a warm squeeze. "I know it's dull around here for you these days with Kerry gone. I don't blame you one bit for wanting something exciting to happen."

Meg didn't say anything.

"I have to leave on a trip early tomorrow. I'll be gone almost a week. I'm sorry I have to go away just now, but when I get back, you and I will start planning a trip. Where would you like to go?''

Meg hesitated. She felt a little excited in spite of herself. She loved trips with her father. They had been to some very exciting places.

''Well . . . I don't know. . . .'' She tried to think.

''All right. Eat your dinner now. You sleep on it tonight. And then in the morning, we'll talk about it before I leave.''

4
THE QUEEN
ON THE HILL

The next morning, Mrs. Wilson had set the table for them in the pleasant dining room alcove. And she had made blueberry biscuits as a special treat because Mr. Duncan was going away.

Meg's father helped himself to another hot biscuit and spread it with butter. "Last night, I called Uncle Hal."

"Has he gone to Maine yet?"

"No, he's still in New York. He's working on some special museum project. But he's going to be in Maine for the whole month of August. He thinks it would be a great idea if we came up. Would you like that?"

Meg put down her fork. "Oh, Daddy—" Her brown eyes shone. "Yes, yes! We can go crabbing, and we can swim and sail. We can look for things that have been washed up on the beach in the storms."

"Storms on the Maine coast are a lot different from the ones here in Virginia, aren't they? Remember that picture Uncle Hal painted of the waves crashing against the black rocks?"

"Yes." Meg's eyes took on their dreaming look. "I'll take my paints. Uncle Hal and I can go off and paint together, the way we did last summer."

"He thinks you have talent. He asked me last night what you have been painting."

"Well, I did one of Thunder. And one of the ballet dancer after you took me to the ballet last winter. Lately I haven't done anything. But I think I know what I'd like to paint. That house. . . ."

"What house?"

"The Haywood house. I'd like to paint it the way

49

it looked in the storm last night. It was like—like a queen, Daddy. An old, raggedy queen sitting on the hill.''

"Raggedy?''

"Yes. That fancy wooden part, where it needs fixing, sort of looks like torn lace.''

"You paint it like that, Meg. And you try to have it all finished to show me when I get back.''

Just as soon as Meg had kissed her father good-bye, she went to get her paints. She was glad she had something interesting to work on while he was gone. The paints were in a real artist's paint box, an old one of Uncle Hal's. It was black tin and big enough to carry everything she needed.

Thunder ran ahead of Meg as she walked into the meadow looking for a spot where she had a good view of the Haywood house. There were so many trees that it was hard to see as much of the house as she had seen from her bedroom window.

But she found a good spot under a shady old apple tree. Thunder played with the little green

apples that had fallen to the ground. Meg got out her sketch pad and pencil. Uncle Hal had told her it was a good idea to make a little drawing first.

She leaned back against the trunk of the apple tree. Yes, it did look like an old queen over there on the hill. And the fancy trimming really looked like torn lace.

Meg made quick lines with her pencil. And then she frowned. Maybe she had better leave out some of the wooden lace. And she had never seen so many windows! She was glad the trees hid most of them. But she did want especially to get those on the third floor just right. The roof, jutting out over them, looked just like eyebrows, and. . . .

Why, how strange . . . one of those windows was being opened!

Meg remembered what the grown-ups had said to her about her imagination. She shut her eyes tight for a moment before she looked again.

But that window was really opening. Slowly, as if somebody might be trying not to make any noise.

52

Did she just imagine she saw somebody standing back from the window? No, she didn't imagine it. There really was somebody there.

This time, she decided, *I am not going to tell a single soul.* She put everything back in the tin box and closed it with a snap. *This time I'm not going to have everybody laughing at me.*

She called to Thunder. He wouldn't come because he was chasing a bee.

Back in her own yard, she walked past Mr. Wilson. He was busy pruning the faded blossoms on the climbing roses. "What have you been doing, Meg?"

"Oh, nothing much."

"Where's Thunder?"

"He's chasing a bee."

He gave a chuckle. "I hope he doesn't catch it." His pruning shears went *snip, snip.*

Meg looked back over her shoulder at him. "Mr. Wilson?"

Snip, snip. "Yes, Meg?"

"I just happened to be up in the meadow. I just

happened to be drawing a picture of the Haywood house. And I would like to have you come and look at something—with your own eyes.''

Mr. Wilson laughed. ''Now, who else's eyes do you think I'd be using?''

''Oh, Mr. Wilson, you know what I mean. I just want you to see for yourself. I don't want you to take my word for it. You know the third floor of the Haywood house, where the servants' rooms used to be?''

''Yes.''

''Well''—she kept her voice calm—''somebody opened a window up there just now. I want you to come and look. With your—''

''With my own eyes. All right, I will. I'm almost finished here.''

''I'll wait right here.''

''No, don't do that. I'm bound and determined I'll get the rest of the lawn mowed before the heat of the day. It's a sight the way the grass has grown since that rain.''

"Oh, dear," said Meg. "It's awfully hard to be patient with you, Mr. Wilson."

She went into the house for some milk and cookies. She took them out on the patio.

Thunder came and jumped onto her lap. He was thirsty. He tried to drink from her glass, and Meg poured some milk into his red dish.

She heard the lawn mower start up, and with a sigh she got out her paints. She set up her easel in the shade and squeezed paint onto her palette. Green for the trees, blue for the sky, white for the wooden trim on the Haywood house. She knew that by the time the lawn was mowed, Mrs. Wilson would have lunch ready.

Sure enough, when the lawn was finished, Mrs. Wilson called them for lunch. And after that, Mr. Wilson had to drive to the village on an errand.

"Oh, Mr. Wilson! You promised!"

"I know. Tell you what I'll do, Meg. You hop into the car with me, and we'll go to the village. Then we'll drive around by the Haywood house. We'll drive up the lane so we can have a good look at those third-floor windows.''

But when they drove up the lane, they saw right away that all the windows on the third floor were closed.

''But one was open, Mr. Wilson,'' Meg insisted. ''Open, open!''

''Okay, okay.'' He reached to tweak her braid. ''And now it's closed, closed.''

When he stopped the car in front of their house, he said teasingly, ''Want me to call Constable Hosey?''

Meg got out of the car without a word. She just hated to seem to be wrong about everything!

5

A FAMILY IN TROUBLE

The next day, Meg had a bright idea. She remembered that her father had a pair of field glasses. She tucked them into the big tin box with her art supplies. Then she went down into the kitchen to make herself a sandwich. She knew she just might be gone past the time for a midmorning snack.

She spread peanut butter on bread.

Mrs. Wilson was cleaning out the pantry cupboard. She looked toward the tin box. "Well, well, you are quite the artist these days. Going to paint for a while, I see."

"Yes, Mrs. Wilson. I'm going up to the meadow.

I'm going to try to have the picture finished before Daddy gets back."

"Oh, that's nice." Mrs. Wilson measured out some fresh shelf paper. "Just be sure to stay where you can hear me if I call."

"I will, Mrs. Wilson. Don't worry about me."

She waved to Mr. Wilson as she went through the backyard. He was working in the vegetable garden.

Today, maybe, she would have something to tell him. But she wasn't going to say another word about anything until she was sure he wouldn't be able to tease her about it.

The big old apple tree was perfect for climbing. Meg got the field glasses out of the tin box and slipped the leather strap around her neck.

Thunder took one leap and was halfway up the trunk. Then he ran out to the end of a limb. He looked back and made that little noise in his throat that meant, "Come with me."

Meg climbed as high as she dared go safely. Then she settled in the crotch of a limb and picked up the glasses. Even without them she could see that the windows on the top floor were open again.

She held the glasses to her eyes and turned the little knob that focused the lenses. She caught her breath. Oh, my goodness! There was somebody in the room. Yes, there really was!

She turned the knob a little more. It was a woman, and she was bending over the bed. There was a man lying on the bed!

"I told you so, Thunder. I told you!"

Thunder glanced up as if to say he had known it all along. Then he went on cleaning his paw.

Slowly Meg moved the glasses downward. Somebody was in the garden in back of the house. A girl, a girl with blond hair that was long and straight. She looked as if she might be a couple of years older than Meg.

"A family. . . ." Meg breathed the words out loud. How strange. But how interesting! Just wait until she told the Wilsons this news!

She climbed down from the tree and put the

glasses back in the tin box. Somehow, all of a sudden, she was in no hurry to go back with this news to the Wilsons. What if they told her to stay away from there?

Mr. Wilson would be almost sure to call up Mr. Hosey this very morning. Mr. Hosey would come then and get that family out of there. That would be the end. And Meg wasn't ready for the end just yet.

She glanced back toward the house just to make sure Mrs. Wilson wasn't watching from the kitchen window. Then she hurried across the meadow, following Cricket Run past the Partlow property until she got to the place where the bridge was out. She crossed Old Bridge Road.

This time she didn't go up the Haywood drive. She made her way up the hill through the tall weeds and bushes. She was very quiet, not wanting anybody to see her just yet.

Meg stood behind a tree. She could see the girl in the garden very clearly now. It wasn't much of a garden anymore, all full of weeds. But the girl was picking something. Her long, blond hair fell over her face. What could possibly be growing in a garden full of weeds?

Asparagus. Yes, Meg knew that asparagus came up every year.

Maybe these people were hungry. Maybe the girl had to come out to find food for her family. Maybe they were starving, even!

Meg said, "There's some rhubarb, too, over there by the old grape arbor."

The girl whirled around, dropping half the asparagus. "Is this your property?"

Meg chewed thoughtfully on a pigtail for a moment. Then she flipped it over her shoulder. "No. But I am a very good friend of the owners."

"And you'll go blabbing to them, I suppose. Naturally, being a little kid."

Meg eyed the strange girl coolly. *If she doesn't want to be friendly, then I don't want to be friendly,* she decided.

"I may," she said to the girl. "I've already had the

63

constable come up here once. The constable happens to be a very good friend of mine, too.''

"We heard somebody tramping around downstairs the day after we came.''

"But I may or I may not have Constable Hosey come again.''

"You want me to get on my knees, I guess, and beg you not to.''

Meg leaned down to pick up Thunder. She petted him, her eyes on the girl. ''You can if you want to. But I'd just like to know who you are and why you're here.''

The girl knelt to pick up the asparagus she had dropped. She straightened and said, ''My name is Abby—Abigail, that is—James.''

"Oh. My name is Meg Duncan.''

"My father is sick. He's upstairs there with my mother.''

"Oh. That's too bad.'' Meg wasn't ready yet to tell Abby that she had just been looking at them with the field glasses.

"We got lost in that storm Sunday night. Remember that storm?"

"Yes, I sure do."

"Well, we got off the main road. When we came to that place down there where the bridge is out, we had to turn around. This was the first driveway we came to, and we came in here to see if we could use the phone. Our car was acting up. Daddy was beginning to be real sick, and we were afraid we weren't going to make it to the next town. He knocked and knocked, but nobody came."

"That's because nobody lives here."

"Do you think I don't know that? There are a whole lot of rolled-up newspapers in the shrubbery at the front. They must be pretty stupid people not to have stopped their paper before they left!"

"They're not stupid." Meg's voice was cool again. She had come up here thinking she might get to be friends with this girl, but now she didn't want to.

"Bud and Sally Haywood own this house, and they are awfully, awfully nice. They just forgot, is all.

66

You're stupid, if you ask me, to just plain move into a house, and—''

"We are not!" Abby's cheeks got red. For a moment she looked as if she might be going to cry. "My father was so sick he just fell there on the porch. We had to drag him, almost, into the house. Do you think it would have been smart to just—just let him lie there in the storm?"

"Oh, no!" Meg shook her head. "I'm sorry. Is he still sick?"

"He's got a high fever."

"Don't you think you ought to call a doctor?"

Abby turned and started to walk away. When she turned back, Meg saw that now there really were tears in her eyes. "Since you're so nosy, we don't have money for a doctor!"

"Oh. . . ." Meg's voice was faint.

"My father lost his billfold when we were coming through Indianapolis. We're from Oklahoma, and Daddy was coming east to talk to a man in Washington about a job. He'll get the job, all right. He's very smart, and I'm not worried about that—"

"Oh, I know." Meg said it quickly. "But first he does have to get well."

"Of course. And he will get well. He's very strong. But he's had this terrible cold for over a week, and getting soaked to the skin that night didn't help him any."

Meg thought back to the night of the storm.

"That night—when he went up on the porch to knock—did he have on something white?"

Abby's mouth flew open. "How did you know?"

Meg turned and pointed. "I live down there— that brick house past the big white house with the holly trees and chimneys. I can see part of this house from my window, through the trees. I was watching the storm, and I saw a car. And then I saw somebody in white—"

"Yes. Daddy had Mother's white plastic raincoat over his shoulders. She's little and he's big, so it didn't do much good with the wind blowing."

"Yes, yes!" Meg said it excitedly. She was glad to

have this much solved. "I could see it—all fluttery—like a ghost. But then the rain came down real hard—"

"I know. And Daddy fell. The door wasn't locked, and Mother and I called and called. We thought there might be somebody in there asleep. Then we looked around for a telephone."

"They had it disconnected."

"Yes, I know. Daddy was too sick by then to go anywhere else. Mother didn't know what else to do, and there was a fireplace in that room with all the books—"

"The library," Meg said.

"Yes. And there was some wood, so Mother and I made a fire. We'll pay for the wood, of course, and everything else just as soon as we can."

Meg said earnestly, "You don't need to. Sally and Bud wouldn't let you. You can just stay on here and not worry about anything."

"You don't own this place. You haven't any right to say we can stay."

69

"I know, but—"

"We're trespassing." Abby stood tall, looking down on Meg. "We've got sense enough to know it's against the law to trespass. That's why we're hoping nobody will find out we're here. That's why Mother had me come down and wash our footprints off the front porch. We'll get thrown out, maybe even put in jail, if anybody catches us . . . anybody who matters."

Meg looked at Abby's unhappy face. "I won't tell anybody."

"Promise?"

"Yes, I promise."

"Swear?"

Meg was getting tired of this. "Listen, I said I promised."

"Oh. Well, all right. Only, everything in my whole life is suddenly going all wrong!" The girl's cheeks got red again, and her blue eyes looked a little too bright. "I never wanted to leave Oklahoma anyhow, but they wouldn't listen. Grown-ups won't ever listen

70

to children! And now look at all the terrible things that have happened.''

Abby started for the house, and Meg fell into step behind her. "If your father needs help, I think it would be better to . . . to. . . .''

"Better to what?" Abby looked around, waiting.

Meg frowned. The tip of her pigtail went into her mouth again. Her father had always told her that policemen were friends. But how could you go to them for help when you were trespassing and breaking the law?

"Oh, dear," she said. "I wish my father were at home. He'd know what you ought to do, Abby."

"You promised not to tell," Abby reminded her. "And that means everybody."

"Everybody?" She had been thinking that maybe she might call her father. "But maybe I ought to try to get you some help."

"No. We don't need any help." Abby started up the steps. Meg could see the open window where she had come out. "By tomorrow, Daddy may be well enough for us to leave. Mother has been giving him lots of aspirin.''

Meg looked up from the bottom of the steps. ''But there are things better than aspirin. They call them, uh, miracle drugs. I could go on my bicycle—''

''You can't just go into a drugstore and say, 'I want some miracle drugs.' My goodness, you ought to know that much. First you have to have a doctor.''

''Oh.'' Meg hadn't known that.

From far away there came the sound of a voice calling, ''Meg . . . Meg. . . .''

''Oh, I've got to go.''

''Hurry.'' Abby's eyes looked frightened. ''Hurry, or they might come looking for you.''

''I know. I'm going.'' Meg started to leave. Then she turned. ''But tell me one more thing. What happened to your car?''

''Mother put it out in back in the shed.''

''Oh.'' Meg started hurrying down the hill.

Abby's voice came after her. ''You're not going to tell, are you? Remember, you promised me!''

"I know. I won't tell."

From down at the house she could hear Mrs. Wilson's voice calling her name again.

"Coming . . . coming, Mrs. Wilson. . . ."

6
A PROMISE IS A PROMISE

Mrs. Wilson was standing at the kitchen door waiting for her when she came back. "Mercy me, where were you, child?"

"Oh, just around." Meg gave a shrug and didn't meet Mrs. Wilson's worried eyes.

"I tried to see you out in the meadow from the kitchen window. And when I couldn't see you, I went out to look for you. I found your paint box with the sandwich still in it, but—"

Meg edged past her. "Oh, I just wasn't very hungry. I just . . . just sort of wandered. You know, up past Mrs. Partlow's place. . . ."

"Well, hurry now and get your hands washed. I have lunch all ready. And after lunch, I think you had just better stay around here. You can sit out on the patio where it's cool and work on your picture. My goodness, child, you're not going to have that picture done by the time your father gets back."

All that afternoon, Meg worried as she painted. The picture of the Haywood house wasn't going very well, but that wasn't what she worried about. She worried about the promise she had made.

Probably if her father had been at home, she would never have made it.

She just couldn't tell the Wilsons, even though maybe that was the right thing to do. They tried so hard to take good care of her. They took care of her, not just because it was their duty, but because they really loved her.

Meg squeezed some fresh paint onto her palette. *My, oh, my, trespassers!* She could just imagine Mrs. Wilson saying it. *Breaking into a house that doesn't*

*belong to them! Why, Meg, we don't know any-
thing about those people. We can't have you wander-
ing off up there talking to strangers!*

Meg painted the house from memory. She could
imagine Mr. Wilson's voice even better. He would
go straight to the phone. *Mr. Hosey,* he would say,
come and arrest these trespassers.

Mr. Wilson came onto the patio with a big basket
of vegetables he had picked for dinner. He turned
on the hose to wash them off. "What's been the matter with you this afternoon, Meg?"

"Nothing."

"Nothing, eh?" He looked at her sharply. "Been
missing Kerry quite a bit, I guess."

"Yes."

"Kerry said for you to exercise her pony. Guess
you sort of forgot about that."

"I will," Meg said. "Some other day."

"Are you sick?" He peered at her.

"No." She knew her voice sounded a little bit
mournful.

He finished washing the vegetables and carried them into the house.

As she sat there, Meg thought about how awful it would be to be sick without a doctor. Every time she was the least bit sick, the Wilsons called the doctor right away. Especially when her father was off on a trip.

Sa-a-y. . . . Meg's eyes got as bright as if she had a high fever. Suddenly she had the most wonderful idea.

She piled everything back into the tin box. The paint was still wet on the picture, so she left it sitting there and went into the house and up to her room. She could hear Mr. and Mrs. Wilson talking in the kitchen.

Talking about her, she would just bet. Wondering what was wrong with her.

Thunder was on the bough of the oak tree outside the window, so she opened it. "Hurry, Thunder. I've got things to do."

From the black tin box Meg chose a stick of red

chalk. She would make spots. Over at the mirror she dotted the red chalk all over her face. She frowned. No, the spots didn't look very real.

She wiped them off and started over again. Maybe she would have just a nice, plain fever. She smoothed the chalk carefully on her forehead and cheeks. She had to smile at herself in the mirror. It looked just exactly as if she had a fever. She could just imagine the doctor saying, *We'll have to give this child some miracle drugs.* And then when the miracle drugs came, she would—

"Meg!" Mrs. Wilson's voice came clearly. "Time to wash up for dinner!"

Meg washed her hands carefully to take away the telltale color. Then she smoothed back her hair with a brush and went downstairs.

When her father was away, she always ate with the Wilsons in the kitchen. And they weren't too fussy about it if she didn't get all dressed up.

She took her place quietly. A nice plate of vegetables and fried chicken was placed before her.

A cup of steaming cocoa was beside her plate. Meg was starved. Everything smelled so good.

But when Mr. Wilson had asked the blessing, Meg just leaned her cheek on her hand.

"Don't you feel well, child?"

"I—I feel all right." Meg said it faintly, not looking up.

"You're not eating. And this morning you didn't eat your sandwich."

Mr. Wilson said, "And she didn't feel like going for a ride on Chappie."

Mrs. Wilson said, "Meg, look at me."

Meg gave a big sigh and turned to look up at Mrs. Wilson.

"Oh, my, oh, my! Oh, my stars alive, Meg, you look as if you have a fever! Let me get the thermometer right away!"

Mr. Wilson took hold of her hand. "Your hand is cool—but maybe you're having a chill. I'll go and find you a sweater."

Mrs. Wilson came with the thermometer and popped it into her mouth. "There now, let that stay in your mouth three minutes." And then she went to help Mr. Wilson find the sweater because Mr. Wilson could never manage to find anything around the house.

Oh, dear, thought Meg as she sat there with the thermometer sticking out of her mouth. She had just thought they would take one look at her pink face and call a doctor right away. This thermometer was going to give her away in just three little minutes. What could she do?

She propped her chin on her hands, and one of her elbows touched the hot cocoa.

Hot . . . yes . . . very hot. . . .

She slipped the thermometer into the cocoa for just a few seconds and had it back in her mouth by the time the Wilsons came back with the sweater.

Mr. Wilson slipped the sweater over Meg's shoulders. Mrs. Wilson took out the thermometer and looked at it.

"My, oh, my!" Her voice sounded frightened. "This child has a temperature of a hundred and six!"

She put her hand on Meg's forehead. And then she peered closely, her eyes narrowed. She took one corner of her white apron and rubbed it over Meg's pink cheek.

"Tsk, tsk, tsk. Look at that." She held up the apron with a smudge of pink. "Margaret Ashley Duncan, you scared me half to death. What did you do with the thermometer—put it in your cocoa?"

Meg nodded. She felt very foolish about the whole thing.

Mrs. Wilson smoothed back Meg's hair. "Well, I guess with your daddy gone you just wanted a little attention, didn't you? With Kerry and all the Carmodys gone, it isn't very exciting around here, is it? Eat your dinner, now."

Mr. Wilson said, "Only don't scare us like that again. Promise?"

"I promise."

Oh, dear, she thought. *Me and all my promises!*

Right now she felt as if she just had to confess everything and tell the Wilsons the whole story. She wished she had never made that promise to Abby not to tell.

She said, "Mrs. Wilson, is it just terrible for a person to break a promise?"

"A promise? Oh, dearie me, yes. A promise is a sacred thing."

Mr. Wilson helped himself to some chicken and more vegetables. Then he turned to look at Meg.

Almost as if he were reading her mind, he said, "Meg, you know you thought something was wrong up at the Haywood house?"

Meg gulped. "I—I did?"

"Why, yes, of course you did. And this afternoon I noticed something strange myself."

"You—you did?" She took a piece of chicken and started eating it.

"Yes. I had a minute to spare, and I walked up there to where the bridge is out—they haven't even started fixing it—and I happened to glance up toward the Haywood house. It's kind of hard to see up there because of all the trees, but it looked like there was an old car parked out in the shed. I wonder what it's doing there. . . ."

"Did—did you go up there?"

"No. I had to get the vegetables picked in time for dinner, and—"

Meg said quickly, "Bud Haywood is just crazy about old cars. He takes them apart and—and everything. . . ."

"I know, I know. But I don't think Bud had that car there before he left. Tomorrow, soon as I get the time, I think I'll just wander up that way and have a look at that car. . . ."

7

MEG TRIES
TO HELP

The alarm went off early the next morning. Meg grabbed it after the first jingle. She didn't want the Wilsons wondering why she had set the alarm to get up so early.

But they just seemed glad she had come down to have breakfast with them. "Well, well, how are you feeling this morning?" Mr. Wilson said with a wink at Mrs. Wilson.

"Fine." Meg slid into her chair. "I'm just going to get an early start this morning, the way you do."

Right after breakfast, Mrs. Wilson went out to sweep off the front steps and walk, the way she always did. She said she liked to "get the smell of the morning."

Meg hurried into the pantry with her black tin box. Maybe she hadn't been able to get any medicine for Mr. James, but she could take him some food.

Quickly she emptied the box of her art supplies. Then she put in as many cans of food as the box would hold. She put in pineapple and tuna fish and soup and some cans of hash and baked beans. She wished the box would hold a whole lot more. But then she lifted it. The box was much heavier than it had been with just the paints and brushes. It was almost too heavy to carry as she hurried out the back door.

Mrs. Wilson's voice came after her as she went down across the lawn toward the meadow. "Now, don't go far, Meg. Come when I call you." And then she said, "Oh, dear, I didn't do your braids!"

"That's all right, Mrs. Wilson." Meg sang the words over her shoulder, not looking back. "They look okay. Anyway, you can do them this noon."

She gave a sigh. Grown-ups were always worrying about little things that weren't important at all. What was important was getting this food over to the James family—and warning them that Mr. Wilson was coming to look at their car.

She went into the meadow. Then, when she was sure Mrs. Wilson was no longer watching, she hurried along Cricket Run, past the Partlow house, across Old Bridge Road, and up the Haywood hill.

Abby wasn't in the garden this morning. Meg picked up some pebbles and threw them at the third-floor windows. Abby's blond head appeared. She waved to Meg and disappeared. In a minute, she climbed out the window onto the front porch.

"What's the matter?" she said.

She looked sleepy, and Meg didn't think she looked much friendlier than she had yesterday.

"We have to take those Oklahoma license plates off your car right away."

"What's the matter with you, Meg? We can't do that."

Meg said earnestly, "Listen. I worried and worried about those license plates, and that's the only thing I can think of to do. Mr. Wilson—that's the man who lives at our house and helps take care of things—is going to come up here today. Yesterday he looked up here and saw your car in the shed. I'm hoping he will think it's Bud Haywood's car. But if he sees those license plates. . . ."

Abby nodded slowly as she understood what Meg was getting at. "That's right."

"That's right." Another voice echoed the words from the window. Abby's mother smiled down at Meg.

Mrs. James had the same blond hair and blue eyes as her daughter, but she seemed friendlier. "You're Meg, aren't you? Abby told me about you yesterday. It's kind of you to try to help us. That's good thinking about the license plates. I thought I had put the car out of the way where nobody would see it."

She turned to Abby. "I want you to go out to the

shed right now, dear, and take those license plates off.''

"But, Mother, I don't know how to take license plates off a car.''

"They're bolted on. I don't think you'll have any trouble. You'll find a screwdriver and pliers in the tool kit. Hurry, dear.''

As Abby went around the corner of the house, Meg said, "Mrs. James, I brought you some things. Just—just in case you couldn't get out to the grocery store. You know, people always take presents to people when they're sick.''

Mrs. James looked down at her for a moment and then laughed. But Meg saw tears in her eyes.

"Why, thank you, Meg. Mr. James is better this morning. But you're right; it is hard for me to get out to the grocery store.''

Mrs. James helped Meg lift the heavy tin box through the window. Out in the kitchen, they emptied it of all the canned food.

Meg said thoughtfully, "Maybe you'd just better

let Abby think you found these things here in the cupboard. I think she sort of has the idea that I'm butting in.''

Mrs. James said, ''I have used a few things from the cupboard. I do plan to pay for them. But I think it would be better if Abby knew you were kind enough to bring us a present.''

And then she put her arm around Meg for a moment in a quick hug. ''Don't mind the way Abby acts. She is just very unhappy about all the trouble we're in. She keeps saying that if we hadn't left Oklahoma, none of this would have happened.''

Meg nodded. ''I think I know how she feels, sort of.''

''Yes, so do I. You see, back home Abby was a very popular girl. She had been elected president of her school class for next year.''

''She—she had?''

''Yes. She was just a different girl back home. This summer she was going to be a junior counselor at the day camp. We all just loved our little town.''

94

"Then why did you leave?"

"Mr. James had a bookstore. It was in a little college town. And when the college was moved away, the little town just began to die."

"I didn't know they moved colleges."

"Yes, sometimes they do. It's good for the college, but it's very hard on the little town that's left behind. Our bookstore just couldn't make a go of it without the college. But Mr. James is pretty sure he can get a good job in Washington."

Meg said earnestly, "Oh, I'm sure everything will be all right, Mrs. James. We just have to get him well real fast."

"I'm not too much worried about him now. But I'd feel so much better about staying here if we could get in touch with the owners."

Meg frowned. "Bud is in Alaska somewhere working in a fish-canning factory. Sally is working in Yellowstone Park."

"Yellowstone Park is a pretty big place. Part of it is in Wyoming, and part of it is in Idaho. And

96

part of it is in Montana, I think.''

"Wait a minute! I just remembered. Sally sent me a postcard with a picture of the place where she's working. The name of the place is on it—sort of a funny name—and the address. I'll hurry home right now and look. And then I can call her up and ask her if it's all right for you to stay here!''

"Oh, Meg, that's wonderful. Have the operator tell you how much it costs. I'll want to pay for it.''

"All right, I will.''

She almost bumped into Abby, who was coming in with the license plates. "What's the hurry?''

"Your mother will tell you. 'Bye. I've got to hurry.''

Carrying the empty tin box, Meg ran down the hill. When she went in her back door, she could hear the vacuum cleaner going and Mrs. Wilson singing. *Oh, good,* she thought. *A break at last.*

Up in her room, she found Sally's card right away. Moosalucky Lodge. And the postmark said Montana.

She went into her father's room, where there was an extension phone. She knew just how to place a person-to-person call, for she had called her father many times. The operator said she would call her back when she had completed the call.

Meg touched a jade carving that sat on her father's desk. He had brought it from Japan. She loved the feeling of the smooth, green stone. "I'm going to sit right here," she vowed. "I'm going to sit right here and not move until that operator calls me back."

But just then she heard Mrs. Wilson's voice from downstairs. "Margaret Ashley Duncan!"

"Oh, brother," Meg breathed. That meant trouble. Every single time Mrs. Wilson used her full name, it meant she had found out about something.

She started down the stairs.

"What on earth are all those brushes and paints and things doing in my clean pantry?"

Oh, dear. Meg had forgotten all about leaving everything in the pantry. "I'll get them, Mrs. Wilson. I'll pick everything up right away."

She got her tin box and hurried to the pantry. Mrs. Wilson followed her. "I thought you went out to paint this morning, Meg. I stood right over there at the kitchen door. You were carrying that box as if it were full of every last thing you owned.''

Meg looked at Mrs. Wilson's puzzled face. *Oh, if I could only tell her,* she thought. Mrs. Wilson would be so glad she had taken the food to somebody who needed it!

The telephone rang. Meg started toward it. "I'll get it."

"No, I will get it." Mrs. Wilson's voice was firm. "You just finish picking up those things."

Meg listened as Mrs. Wilson picked up the kitchen phone. In a moment, Mrs. Wilson turned, holding the phone. She had a strange look on her face. "Meg, did you place a call to *Montana?*"

"Yes, I did." Meg rushed to take the phone from Mrs. Wilson's hand. "Hello—hello—"

"I am sorry"—the operator's voice was just as polite as if she were talking to a grown-up—"the party you called cannot be reached. Will you speak with anyone else?"

"No. But you just keep trying, and when you get her, you call me. Thank you." Meg put back the phone. She waited a moment before she turned around to face Mrs. Wilson.

Mrs. Wilson said, "Who on earth do you know in Montana, Meg?"

"Sally."

"But why would you need to call Sally?"

"I—I just have to talk to her about something."

"Long-distance calls cost money, child."

"Daddy wouldn't mind. I'll tell him all about it when he comes home. He won't mind at all. He'll be *glad* I called Sally."

Meg threw her arms around Mrs. Wilson. "And I'll tell you, too, but not right now. Oh, please, Mrs. Wilson, I just can't tell you right now!"

"Meg, you're not solving anything, are you? The way you did when Mrs. Partlow's diamonds disappeared?"

"No. Truly. I'm not solving anything."

Mrs. Wilson smoothed Meg's untidy braids. "My,

oh, my. I just don't like this one bit. Suppose you run upstairs now and get your brush and comb. Then while I do your hair, we can talk about it some more."

Meg got her brush and comb and came back with slow steps. "It's a promise I made, Mrs. Wilson. I promised I wouldn't tell. And last night you told me that a promise is sacred. That's exactly what you said."

"I know, but—"

"I'll tell you everything when Sally calls me. Honest. And that's a promise, too. I'm sure Sally will be calling me back today."

But Meg waited all afternoon, and Sally did not call.

That night at dinner Mr. Wilson said, "About that car in the Haywood shed. . . ."

Meg stopped chewing. She stopped swallowing. She almost stopped breathing.

"Yes, what about it?" said Mrs. Wilson. She was pouring some more milk into Meg's glass.

"Well, I went up there this afternoon. The car is there, all right. But it has no license plates. It's not worth much. So I guess maybe Bud did leave it there."

Meg breathed deeply and reached for her glass of milk.

That night, just before she went to bed, she went again to the phone on her father's desk. This time she told the operator she would speak to anyone who answered.

In a couple of minutes, a friendly western voice was saying that Sally had gone on a two-day pack trip. She was expected back tomorrow night by seven-thirty at the latest. Yes, ma'am, he would see to it that Sally Haywood called Miss Margaret Duncan right away.

....
8
*FOOTSTEPS IN
THE NIGHT*
....

All that next day, the Wilsons watched Meg like a pair of hawks. Something was up. They knew it. And they didn't like it.

I just have to get out of this house somehow to tell the James family about Sally, Meg worried. She could do it in fifteen minutes. She could even do it in ten minutes if she flew!

She said, "I guess I'll go out into the meadow and paint."

"Fine," said Mrs. Wilson, starting to untie her apron. "I believe I'll just go along with you. The wild strawberries are probably ripe there now."

So Meg decided she wouldn't go to the meadow.

A little later, she got out her bike. Mr. Wilson was working around the boxwood hedge at the front. "Where are you going, Meg?"

"I'm just going to ride my bike for a while."

"Good. Just ride up and down Culpepper Road. And stay where I can see you. Don't go past Mrs. Partlow's."

Meg rode up the road to the corner of the Partlow house. She rested a minute, looking in the direction of the Haywood house on the hill. There was nothing much to be seen from here. The trees hid the windows on the third floor.

I'm just like a prisoner, she thought, *a prisoner until tonight when Sally calls.*

Mrs. Partlow was on her lawn cutting some roses. She called, "What are you looking at, Meg?"

"Nothing." Meg wheeled the bicycle over to the edge of Mrs. Partlow's lawn. She watched as Mrs. Partlow dropped the roses, white like her hair, into the basket. "What are you going to do with the

105

roses, Mrs. Partlow?'' Meg asked.

"I'm going to take them to a friend who is ill."

"Oh." Meg studied her for a moment. She was so kind. And even though she was sort of old, she did like a bit of excitement. Of all the neighbors, Meg felt that Mrs. partlow was the only one she might be able to explain things to.

But a promise was a promise.

"Good-bye, Mrs. Partlow." Meg got on her bike and slowly rode home. She was just going to have to wait until tonight when Sally would call. Seven-thirty, the man had said. At the latest.

It was after lunch that Mrs. Wilson found out the pineapple was missing.

Meg was out on the patio, trying to paint clouds so they would look real. In the kitchen, she heard Mrs. Wilson say to Mr. Wilson, "I just know I had a can of pineapple in this pantry. Meg was in here yesterday, and—"

"Now, you know Meg wouldn't eat a whole can of

pineapple. She couldn't.'' Mr. Wilson was sitting in there having his pipe and his after-lunch rest.

"I know, but it's very strange, very strange indeed. I did want that pineapple for a dessert I was going to make for dinner tonight.''

"If you were going to make a pineapple upside-down cake, I'll be glad to go to the store.'' Meg knew that Mr. Wilson was just wild about pineapple upside-down cake.

"All right. And I have a list of some other things you can get.'' Mrs. Wilson lowered her voice, but Meg could still hear her. "Why don't you take Meg with you? Poor child, here all alone, nobody to play with. . . .''

Mr. Wilson came out on the patio. "Meg, I have to go to the store. Would you like to go with me?''

Meg started cleaning off her paintbrush. "Yes, I guess so.'' Going to the store wasn't much fun, but it was better than nothing.

Then Mr. Wilson said, "I think maybe I might drop you by the Carmody place. There's a man taking care of things at the barn. You could ride Kerry's pony; Chappie needs to be exercised. I have some errands in Hidden Springs that will take me about an hour.''

An hour! A whole hour!

Meg felt free as the wind when she was on Chappie's back. Mr. Wilson had cautioned her to ride just around the meadow. Meg hated to disobey, but this was so important. Even the Wilsons, when she told them tonight, would agree.

Meg galloped around the back road. Chappie waded easily through Cricket Run where the workmen were just beginning to repair the stone bridge that was out. She knew one of the men. He told her it would be two or three days before the bridge was finished.

When she reached the Haywood house, Abby came right out, as if she had been expecting her.

Meg tied Chappie to a tree, and Abby said, ''We wondered what happened to you. Come in. Mother wants to talk to you.''

The two girls climbed in the window. "Come on upstairs," Abby said. "You haven't met my father yet. He's lots better today."

Meg liked Mr. James the minute she saw him. He was tall and thin. He had his clothes on, but he was still lying on the bed. He had a smile like Abby's —not that Meg had seen Abby smile very many times.

"So you're Meg. I've been wanting to meet you. We are very grateful to you. I had a whole can of soup for my lunch, and pineapple is my favorite fruit."

Meg said she was glad. Mrs. James said, "Did you call your friend?"

Meg told what she had found out. "But I'm sure she will call tonight by seven-thirty. You really don't have anything to worry about."

Abby said unhappily, "But now we have something new to worry about."

"You do?"

"Yes. Last night we heard footsteps downstairs."

110

Meg could feel her eyes widen. "Was it the police?"

"No," Mr. James said. He propped himself up on the bed. "Definitely not the police. Whoever it was moved very quietly."

"But there's nothing here worth stealing."

"I don't think he stole anything. There wasn't time. Abby was leaning against this door up here, listening. She leaned too hard and slammed it shut. The man, I think, was frightened away. He left in a hurry through one of the windows. We looked out and caught just a glimpse of him through the trees as he ran down the hill. And then we heard a car motor start up."

"My goodness," Meg breathed.

Mrs. James said, "This morning I went down and had a good look around. There seemed to be some books out of place in the library."

Meg's eyes got even bigger. "Maybe he was looking for a secret door or something like that, behind the books—"

112

"Secret door!" Abby gave a scornful laugh. "Real houses don't have secret doors. Just houses in books."

Mr. James looked worried. "We know we should get in touch with the police, but how can we just yet? Meg, I wish that friend of yours would hurry up and call."

"I'm sure Sally will call tonight. And as soon as she does, I'll come right up here."

She didn't dare stay any longer now. Abby went downstairs with her.

Meg said, "If anything comes up—you know, anything important—you can just. . . ." Her voice trailed off as she looked into Abby's blue eyes.

"I can just what?"

"Well, I did read this in a book, Abby. But it might be a good idea. If you want to signal me, or . . . or anything, just put something white in the attic window."

But Abby didn't laugh. "I think I read that same book. It was real good, I thought. But then I was only a little kid when I read it. . . ."

A little kid, indeed, Meg thought as she started off. *Hmph*. She didn't like Miss Abby James very much.

"Don't fall off that pony!" Abby said it just loud enough for Meg to hear her.

Meg turned to say crossly that she had never yet fallen off, but Chappie chose that moment to break into a gallop, and Meg slid off to the ground.

Furious, she picked herself up. She heard Abby say, "Are you hurt? Oh, I'm sorry." She sounded

114

sorry enough, but Meg pretended she hadn't heard her.

Chappie came trotting back, as if to say he was sorry, too. Meg jumped on his back and rode very fast down the hill.

She couldn't *stand* that Abby James!

9

WHITE IN THE WINDOW

There was a pineapple upside-down cake that night for dinner. Mr. Wilson had two helpings. Meg kept listening for the phone, hoping her call would come early.

"Have some more dessert, Meg?"

"No, thank you. It was awfully good. I think I'll go upstairs and read for a while."

Meg got her book. She went into her father's room and curled up in his big leather chair, the way she often did when she was reading.

It was a very good book, all about a family that searched for buried treasure. But Meg just couldn't keep her mind on it. She kept waiting for the phone to ring.

She knew what Sally would say. She would say that the James family was welcome to stay at the house. "And then," Meg planned, "I'll rush right downstairs and tell the Wilsons all about everything."

Mr. Wilson might think he ought to call up Mr. Hosey about the prowler that had been in the Haywood house last night. But that would be all right. By then the James family would have permission to stay there. Oh, it was going to be such a relief when Sally called!

But the phone didn't ring.

At about eight-thirty, Meg gave up. She might as well get ready for bed, even though it wasn't dark yet.

She went to her own room and put on her pajamas. Then she went over to the window to let Thunder come in. Climbing the big oak tree was fun for Thunder. As he jumped into her arms, Meg looked toward the Haywood house. She remembered that

117

night of the storm, when she had seen that figure in white, unable to believe her eyes.

She leaned forward, almost doubting her eyes again. There was something white hanging from the third-floor window! The sun had gone down, but the reflected light showed it clearly. A signal!

"Oh, dear. Thunder, what shall I do?" Meg looked into his big blue eyes. He purred at her.

"You're no help." She put him down and pressed her hands over her eyes, trying to think. If only Sally had called. But now she probably wasn't going to call; she knew what time Meg had to go to bed.

And I still can't tell the Wilsons, worried Meg.

She could hear Mrs. Wilson coming up the stairs now. Meg jumped into bed and pulled up the sheet. When Mrs. Wilson came in, she was lying there with her braids prim on her shoulders, holding her book.

Mrs. Wilson leaned to kiss her good night. "Turn off your light in a few more minutes, Meg. Mr. Wilson and I are going to bed pretty soon. We're tired."

"Good night, Mrs. Wilson. Sleep well." *And*

119

quickly, please, Meg added to herself. For she knew now exactly what she was going to do.

Meg waited until she was sure the Wilsons would have gone to bed. Hurriedly then, she put on her blue jeans and a dark shirt. And very quietly she opened the screen and climbed out onto the branch of the big oak tree.

She had climbed down this tree many times, just for fun. This time she was extra careful, not wanting to make a single sound.

It was dark now, except for the moonlight. But Meg knew every step of the way, and she wasn't afraid. In five minutes, she was standing beside the big, dark Haywood house, tossing pebbles at the third-floor window.

Mr. James's head appeared. "My goodness, Meg. Is that you? Abby will be down right away with a flashlight. But you shouldn't have come up here this time of night."

Mrs. James said the same thing when Meg got upstairs. There was only the feeble gleam of the flashlight that was almost burned out, and even that was carefully shaded. "It just wasn't important enough for you to come up here at night, Meg."

"But I saw the white signal in the window as I was going to bed."

"Yes, Abby put the white towel in the window soon after you had left. I guess you didn't think to look for it. But now that you're here, we'll tell you the news, and you can get right back home."

Mr. James said, "I think I figured out what it was that the prowler was looking for last night."

"You did?"

"Yes." He turned to Abby. "Go into the other room and get the book, dear. Handle it carefully."

"Book?" In the dim room, Meg turned puzzled eyes from one face to the other.

"Yes. There's nothing downstairs among those books that's worth anything much. I've looked them over—and I do know something about books." He took the book Abby held out. "But Abby happened to bring this one upstairs the day after we came. I hadn't even seen it until this afternoon.''

Meg looked at the small, paperbound book Mr. James was holding in his hands. It didn't look like much of a book to her. But he was holding the book as if it were solid gold.

"Meg, did you ever hear of Edgar Allan Poe?"

"Y-Yes. We had some of his poems at school. They're beautiful and sort of sad."

"Yes. He lived here in Virginia more than a hundred years ago. Everybody in this state should be very proud of him. He wrote some of the greatest mystery stories that have ever been written. This is a first edition of one of his books, *The Murders in the Rue Morgue*. It may be worth as much as twenty-five thousand dollars."

Meg breathed, "Twenty-five thousand dollars. . . ." And then she gasped, "Oh! That man. . . ."

"That man?"

"That mean old antique dealer. He kicked Sally Haywood's dog."

The three of them were looking at her, waiting

for her to go on. She told them about the little man with the hunched-up shoulders who had tried to buy everything in the house for fifty dollars.

"I bet he saw that book then, Mr. James. He knew Sally was going away for the summer. And I bet last night he came back to try to steal it."

Mr. James nodded. "I wouldn't be a bit surprised. That makes sense to me, all right."

Slowly Meg said, "And to think that for years, maybe, it's just been sitting there on that shelf. A real treasure. A treasure nobody even saw."

"Except my daddy." Abby looked at him with pride. There was happiness on her face, a happiness Meg had never seen there before.

"And the antique dealer," said Mr. James, "if your guess is right, Meg."

Mrs. James said, "I'm so happy about it. You were saying Bud and Sally needed money, Meg. Now they can sell the book and have enough money to finish college."

"Now I'll really have something to tell Sally when

she calls," Meg said. "She never did call me tonight at seven-thirty when I thought she would. But in the morning—"

Abby said, "There's two hours' difference in time between here and Montana. We had that last year in geography." But Abby didn't say it with scorn as she might once have done.

"Two hours?"

"Yes, three if you count daylight saving," said Mr. James.

Meg's hands flew to her mouth. "Oh! Wouldn't it be awful if Sally calls while I'm gone? The Wilsons would answer the phone, and they'd find out I was gone—and—oh, boy, I'd better hurry!"

"Yes." Mr. James got up. "And I'm going to walk back with you. I don't like the idea of girls your age being out after dark."

"But aren't you sick anymore?"

"I'm lots better. It might do me good to get out of doors a bit." He turned to his daughter. "Here, put the book away carefully, Abby."

125

Meg said, "Do you think there's any chance of the man coming back?"

"He just might, sometime. We'll keep the book safe up here tonight. And then tomorrow, we'll have to do something about turning it over to somebody else. It ought to be in a bank vault, maybe. I'm going to see about it first thing in the morning. Come along, Meg."

10
THE THIEF COMES BACK

Carefully, Meg and Mr. James made their way, the dimming flashlight barely showing them the narrow stairs. When they were in the hall on the second floor, Mr. James turned off even that feeble glow. Moonlight was coming in the windows, and they could see pretty well.

But it was spooky. Meg held Mr. James's hand. She was glad he had come with her.

The stairs leading to the first floor were broad, with carpeting. Their feet made no sound. At the bottom of the stairs, Mr. James stopped, his hand on Meg's shoulder. He seemed to be listening. He whispered, "Did you hear that, Meg?"

"I—I heard something. Maybe my cat followed me."

"No, it's not a cat. Sh-h-h. I think somebody is on the front porch."

There was another sound, clearer now. Somebody was opening a window.

"Here—hide." Mr. James drew Meg behind the heavy velvet curtain between the hall and the library. The brass rings made a small sound, and Meg held her breath.

In a moment, they could hear footsteps coming softly across the floor. Someone passed very close to them. And then they could hear the sound of books being moved about on the library shelves.

Without a sound, Meg drew back a fold of the drapery and peeked out. It was the little man! The little man with the hunched-up shoulders who had kicked Sally's dog!

He had a small flashlight in his hand. Meg saw him pull out a couple of books to look at them. He muttered under his breath and tossed them aside.

With a great clatter of brass rings, the old curtain fell. Meg and Mr. James were caught in its dusty folds.

The little man ran. Mr. James reached out and grabbed his leg, but the man gave a kick and got away. Meg got to her feet just in time to see him go through the living-room window. She ran to the window with Mr. James right behind her. She could see the man running through the bushes down over the hill. She screamed, "Help! Stop, thief! Police!"

Down on Old Bridge Road, a car door slammed, and a motor started up with a roar.

Meg scrambled through the window, stumbled, and fell right into the arms of Mr. Wilson. She was so glad to see him she didn't know what to do. "Oh, Mr. Wilson! You've got to stop that man!"

There was a crashing sound down on the road. Mr. Wilson said grimly, "He's stopped, I think. Sounded to me like his car went right through that place where the bridge is out. And I've already

called the police to tell them you were gone. Meg, for goodness' sake, what's the meaning of all this?''

Mr. James was climbing through the window, and Mr. Wilson whirled around to face him.

''I think I can explain,'' said Mr. James. ''But it may take some time. We ought to go and see what's happening to that man.''

They started down the hill. Mrs. James and Abby were now hurrying behind them. When they were halfway down the hill, they saw the flashing light of the police car going along Old Bridge Road. They saw it stop where the bridge was out.

When they came closer, they could see Mr. Hosey helping the little man out of the car that had gone into Cricket Run. In the moonlight, they could see his twisted face look up at Mr. Hosey. He jerked away and ran, but Mr. Hosey caught him easily.

''Hey—what's your hurry?''

Meg broke away from Mr. Wilson's hand. ''Mr. Hosey—Mr. Hosey—I can tell you. He broke into the Haywood house—''

131

"Breaking and entering, eh?" Mr. Hosey looked down at the little man.

"And he was trying to steal—"

"Attempted robbery, eh?" Mr. Hosey took out a pair of handcuffs and snapped them on.

The little man whined, "But I can explain everything."

"Good," said Mr. Hosey. "Come along with me, and I'll give you a chance to explain everything."

They all stood there as the police car drove away. They saw then that Mrs. Partlow had come out to watch, and that Mrs. Wilson was hurrying across the road.

"My, oh, my," she panted. "Margaret Ashley Duncan, come here to me." She hugged her close. "Are you really all right?"

"Yes, yes. Did Sally call?"

"Yes. But what does that have to do with anything?"

"A whole lot. I'll explain later." Then she said politely, "I don't think everybody has met everybody.

Mr. and Mrs. Wilson, I would like to have you meet my friend, Mr. James. And Mrs. James. And Abby. They have been staying in the Haywood house.''

Mrs. Partlow came hurrying across the road. ''And I'm Mrs. Partlow. How do you do? I just had to get in on all the excitement. We haven't had anything this exciting happen in this neighborhood for a long time. Why don't you all come right over to my house? We'll find something to eat. And then we can get acquainted and hear the whole story.''

It was a marvelous party. Everybody forgot all about being tired. Mr. James seemed to forget about being sick. And Meg completely forgot that she hadn't liked Abby very well.

They sat and giggled together. And Meg said she was going to call Sally first thing in the morning and see if it would be all right for the James family to stay in the Haywood house all the rest of the summer.

When all the excitement was over, and all the stories had been told three or four times, Mr. and Mrs. Wilson took Meg home. Everyone started to settle down for the night again.

Meg yawned. She cuddled Thunder beside her. "It was all pretty nice how it turned out, wasn't it, Mrs. Wilson?"

Mrs. Wilson tucked the covers around her. "My, oh, my. Yes, I guess so."

"And it was nice about Mrs. Partlow knowing somebody in Washington to help Mr. James find a job, wasn't it?"

"Yes, that was very nice, Meg. But promise me something."

"What?"

She leaned to give Meg a kiss. "Just promise me that from now on you'll stay out of trouble."

"Well, I'll try, Mrs. Wilson." And then she remembered something. "I think in August, maybe, Daddy and I are going to Maine to visit Uncle Hal."

"Good." Mrs. Wilson said it thankfully. She turned out the light. "I declare, I do need a vacation."

"But you and Mr. Wilson will stay here."

"I know."

"Oh. You mean a vacation from me?"
But Mrs. Wilson had gone down the hall.
Poor Mrs. Wilson. My, oh, my.
Meg smiled as she turned over to go to sleep.

YOU WILL ENJOY

THE TRIXIE BELDEN SERIES

28 Exciting Titles

THE MEG MYSTERIES

6 Baffling Adventures

ALSO AVAILABLE

Algonquin
Alice in Wonderland
A Batch of the Best
More of the Best
Still More of the Best
Black Beauty
The Call of the Wild
Dr. Jekyll and Mr. Hyde
Frankenstein
Golden Prize
Gypsy from Nowhere
Gypsy and Nimblefoot
Lassie—Lost in the Snow
Lassie—The Mystery of Bristlecone Pine
Lassie—The Secret of the Smelters' Cave
Lassie—Trouble at Panter's Lake
Match Point
Seven Great Detective Stories
Sherlock Holmes
Shudders
Tales of Time and Space
Tee-Bo and the Persnickety Prowler
Tee-Bo in the Great Hort Hunt
That's Our Cleo
The War of the Worlds
The Wonderful Wizard of Oz